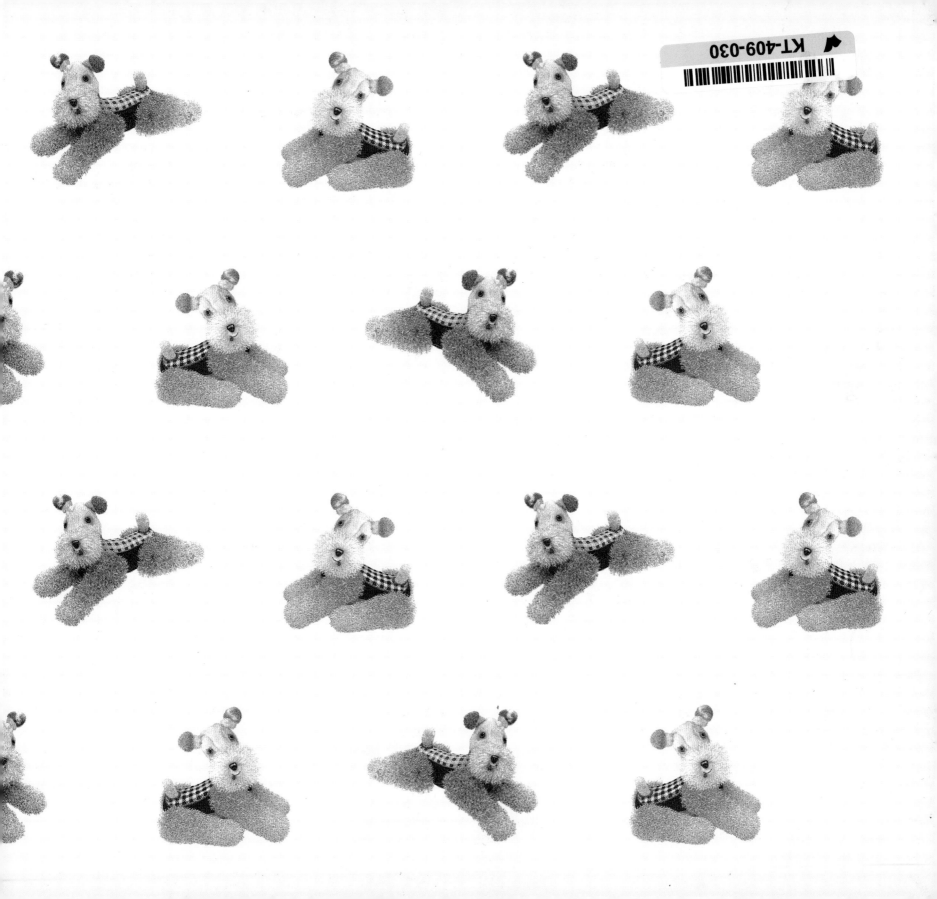

Jane Hissey
RUFF

TED SMART

Old Bear, Bramwell Brown and Little Bear had stopped to listen to a strange noise.
'It's something outside the door saying "Ruff, ruff",' said Old Bear.
'I think I'd better take a look.'

Old Bear carefully opened the door and in bounced a woolly dog. It almost knocked Little Bear off his feet but Duck caught him just in time.

'Hello,' said Old Bear. 'Who are you?'

'I'm a dog,' said their visitor.

'We guessed that,' said Little Bear straightening his trousers, 'but what's your name?'

'I don't think I've got one,' said the dog, trying to look at his collar and bouncing on Duck's toes.

'We could call you Ruff,' said Little Bear. 'Old Bear said he heard a Ruff outside.'

'I like that,' said the dog. 'Does everyone have a name?'

'I think so,' said Little Bear and he took Ruff off to meet the other toys.

'Do you all live here?' asked Ruff.
'*We* do,' said Duck. 'Where do *you* live?'

'I don't know,' said Ruff. 'I was left in the garden next door. I don't think anyone really wants me.'

'I wonder why,' muttered Duck, looking at the muddy footprints Ruff had left all over the floor.

'Perhaps it was because I was rather bouncy,' said Ruff. 'When I was younger,' he added quickly.

'You still are,' grumbled Duck.

Ruff sat down quickly to keep his paws still.

'Everyone's bouncy when they're young,' said Little Bear kindly. 'How old are you now, Ruff?'

Ruff counted his paws, 'One, two, three, four.' Then he added his ears, 'Five, six …' and finally his nose. 'Seven,' he said. 'I think I'm seven.'

'Don't you *know*?' said Little Bear. 'I always count my *birthdays*.'

Ruff said that was a good idea but he'd never had a birthday so there was nothing to count.

'Never had a birthday?' chorused the others. 'Why not?'

'Nobody ever gave me one,' said Ruff.

'That's dreadful,' said Little Bear. 'Old Bear has had hundreds.'

'If you can stay the night with us,' said Bramwell Brown, 'we could give you a birthday tomorrow.'

'Better still,' said Old Bear, 'we could give Ruff *seven* birthdays; one for every year he's missed.'

'An all-week birthday,' said Rabbit. 'Whoopee!'

'Does that mean I can stay for seven nights?' asked Ruff hopefully.

'Of course,' said Old Bear. 'And you can sleep on our bed if you like.'

'As long as you don't bounce,' said Duck.

The next day was Monday and it was Ruff's first birthday.

'Happy birthday, Ruff,' cried all the toys as he jumped down from the bed.

He was soon wearing a special birthday bow that Little Bear had given him.

The others gave him presents too: a rubber bone, a new collar, two pairs of Wellington boots and three balls.

Bramwell Brown had made a beautiful birthday cake.

'That smells delicious,' said Ruff but he sniffed just a little too closely and some of the icing stuck to his nose.

'Ah-tish-ooo!' He sneezed so hard that he blew out the candle on his cake. But the others thought he meant to blow it out so they sang 'Happy birthday to Ruff'.

It's nice to have friends to share a cake with, thought Ruff.

On Tuesday it was Ruff's second birthday.

'Let's play treasure hunts with Ruff's birthday presents,' suggested Little Bear.

Ruff wasn't sure this was a good idea.

'Couldn't we use something else for treasure?' he asked. 'I haven't had my presents very long.'

'I could just hide the three balls then,' suggested Little Bear.

It was great fun treasure hunting and they quickly found two of the balls but nobody could find the third. It was only when Little Bear discovered he couldn't sit down for tea that he remembered he'd hidden it down his trousers.

'I thought they were a bit lumpy,' he said.

Ruff's cake had two candles on it. He blew them out very carefully.

Only five days to go, he thought sadly. I wish I could stay longer.

On Wednesday it was Ruff's third birthday. All his new friends gave him cards they had made themselves. Ruff read them over and over again: the right way up, upside down, inside out and back to front. Then he put them in a row to admire them all together.

Zebra arrived with Ruff's birthday cake. 'Are you ready to blow out your candles?' she said.

Ruff took a deep breath and blew 'Whoooooooo!'

Out went the candles and down went the cards.

What a lot of cards, thought Ruff happily. That's how many friends I have. And he propped them up all over again!

On Thursday it was Ruff's fourth birthday.

'We'll play musical chairs,' said Old Bear, 'with cushions.'

'Mmm, cushions are better for bouncing on,' said Ruff, testing them one by one.

Duck moved out of the way quickly. 'I think I'd rather play the music,' he said.

When he stopped playing, everyone sat on a cushion, except Ruff who landed on Rabbit by mistake.

'I think you're out, Ruff,' said Little Bear. But they let him play to the end of the game anyway because it was his birthday.

Ruff only had enough puff to blow out three of the candles on his cake but he wagged his tail so hard that the last one went out too.

'You can never have as much fun as this on your own,' said Ruff.

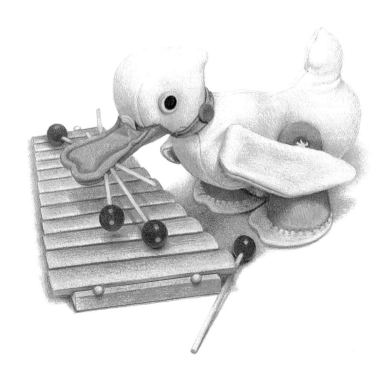

On Friday it was Ruff's fifth birthday.
'I thought we could play pass the parcel today,' said Old Bear,
showing the toys a huge lumpy package he had wrapped up specially.

The toys all sat in a circle and passed the parcel round and round.
When the music stopped whoever was holding the parcel opened one
layer of the paper.

But when it was Ruff's turn he was so excited he tore off all the paper
to reach the prize in the middle.

'That was not playing properly,' said Old Bear crossly.

Ruff's tail drooped. 'I'm sorry,' he said and to show just how sorry he was he let everyone play with his prize *and* blow out the candles on his cake.

'Can I still have another birthday tomorrow?' he asked.

'Only if you are good,' said Old Bear.

On Saturday it was Ruff's sixth birthday. He tried to be very good. He blew up lots of balloons and didn't bounce at all.

Old Bear couldn't think of any more games, so they asked Ruff what he would like to do.

'Well, I've always wanted to drive a train,' he said hopefully.

The little wooden train was too small to fit everyone in so they made a bigger one out of cardboard boxes and string.

'All aboard!' cried Ruff, jumping in. He was in such a hurry to drive off that he nearly forgot Little Bear.

When the train stopped they all had a piece of Ruff's birthday cake. Ruff counted the candles. 'One, two, three, four, five, six . . . Oh dear,' he sighed.

'What's the matter?' asked Little Bear.

'Tomorrow will be my last birthday,' said Ruff sadly.

'Not really,' said Old Bear. 'After tomorrow you'll have one birthday every year, just like the rest of us.'

It would be nice to be like everyone else, thought Ruff.

On Sunday it was Ruff's seventh birthday but when he woke up there seemed to be nobody there.

'Perhaps they've all forgotten me,' he sighed. 'Or maybe they want me to go.'

Sadly he gathered up his new collar, his rubber bone and the three balls and wrote a note saying, 'Thank you for a lovely time, love Ruff.'

He put on his shiny new boots and went to the door. It was then he heard a funny noise out in the hall. Opening the door a tiny crack he peeped out. And there were all his friends.

'Surprise, surprise!' they said. 'Happy Birthday, Ruff. We have a special present for you.' And they brought in a beautiful cushion decorated with all Ruff's favourite things.

'We'd like you to stay with us, Ruff, and this is your very own place to sleep,' said Little Bear.

'Oh thank you,' said Ruff, jumping straight into the middle of his present. 'Now that this is my new home I'll be able to give you birthday surprises too.'

And they all agreed that Ruff's seventh birthday was the happiest one of all.

For James

A TED SMART Publication 1997

'Ruff' birthday cards
designed by Alison Hissey

First published in 1994
© Jane Hissey 1994

First published in the United Kingdom in 1994 by
Hutchinson Children's Books
20 Vauxhall Bridge Road
London SW1V 2SA

Random House UK Limited Reg. No 954009

A CIP catalogue record for this book
is available from the British Library

ISBN: 0 09 176487 4

Printed in Singapore

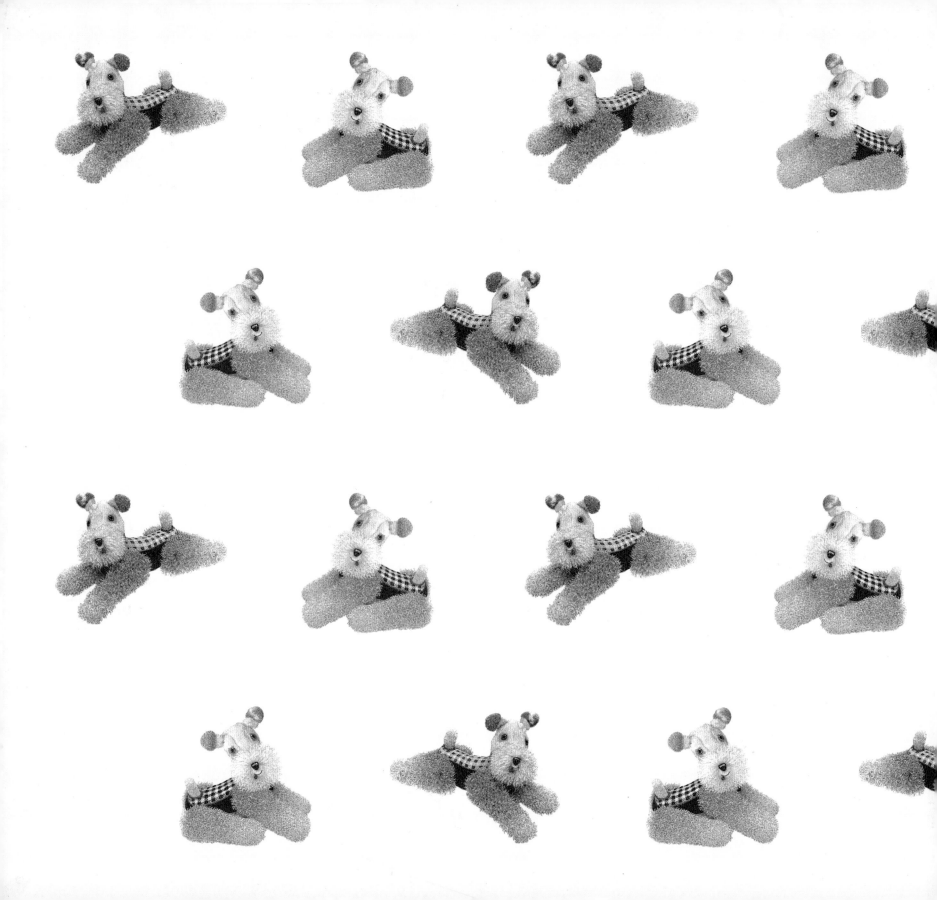